The Magic School Bus

and the Climate Challenge

In memory of Craig Walker,
whose brilliant vision for making science exciting
and funny inspired the Magic School Bus series—
and both of us.
He was much loved, and is much missed.
—J.C. and B.D.

The Magic School Bus

and the Climate Challenge

By Joanna Cole

Illustrated by Bruce Degen

RECYCLED PAPER

Scholastic Inc.

Many have helped in the making of this book. In particular, our sincere thanks go to

Dr. Bill Chameides, Dean and Nicholas Professor of the Environment, Duke University,

for his enthusiastic and informed review.

This book was originally published in hardcover by Scholastic Press in 2010.

ISBN 978-0-545-65599-6

12 11 10 9 8 7 6 5   16 17 18 19/0

Printed in the U.S.A. 40
This edition first printing, January 2014

The text type was set in 15-point Bookman Light.
The illustrator used pen and ink, watercolor, color pencil, and gouache for the paintings in this book.
The text of this book prints on 100% post-consumer recycled fiber.

To all our friends in Korea.
We will never forget your warm and enthusiastic
welcome to The Magic School Bus, and to us.
— J.C. and B.D.

WELCOME, JOON

OUR VISITOR FROM
SOUTH KOREA

Have you heard about our teacher, Ms. Frizzle? Almost every day, something weird happens in her class.

6

For example, take the day we started to study global warming. We were going to put on a play about Earth and all the changes that are happening.

The Friz had brought a book from home, and we were using the pictures to help us paint the scenery.

WHAT IS GLOBAL WARMING?
by Carlos

Global warming is a rise in the average temperature of the land and water on Earth. Today, the average temperature is more than 1 degree F warmer than it was 100 years ago.

One degree doesn't sound like much, but one small degree has caused big changes already— ice melting, seas rising, and more freak weather!

"Ms. Frizzle's book is kind of old," said Tim. "It came out before things really started heating up." "I'll go online to get new pictures," said Wanda. She headed for a computer, but Ms. Frizzle was already out the door. "Come on, class," she called. "Bring my book, please."

LET'S GET REALLY UP-TO-DATE INFORMATION.

I HATE IT WHEN SHE SAYS STUFF LIKE THAT.

WELL, I'VE HEARD HER NAME IS VALERIE....

BUT I CAN'T BELIEVE SHE WAS EVER NINE!

LET'S GO!

OUR WONDERFUL WORLD

This book belongs to Valerie Frizzle. age 9.

Before you could say "North Pole,"
the Friz herded us onto the bus.
She pushed a few buttons and pulled a few levers.
Then we were on our way to the Arctic Sea—
a place with a completely different climate.

MELTDOWN
by Shirley

Melting is happening at the Arctic, Greenland, and the Antarctic.
It's also happening on mountaintops, like the ones in Glacier National Park.

ARCTIC
GLACIER NATIONAL PARK
GREENLAND
NORTH AMERICA
PACIFIC OCEAN
ATLANTIC OCEAN
ANTARCTIC

When we got there, Dorothy Ann opened
Ms. Frizzle's old book.
The pictures showed ice everywhere.
There was still plenty of ice in the Arctic,
but a lot had melted, and more
was melting all the time.

THE ARCTIC... ICE EVERYWHERE!

BY THE TIME WE GROW UP...

...IT MAY BE CALLED GLACIER-**LESS** NATIONAL PARK.

BOULDER GLACIER, Glacier National Park

1932

TODAY

HOW IT LOOKED **THEN**

MELTING CAUSES MORE MELTING
by Tim

Ice is white. White reflects most of the sunlight that hits it. So the sun can't heat up the ice.

Water is not white. It absorbs most of the sunlight that hits it. So the water gets warmer.

SUN

ICE REFLECTS

WATER ABSORBS

This starts a dangerous loop:
- The warm water melts more ice.
- That means there is more water.
- This water takes in more sunlight.
- So the water gets warmer and melts even more ice.

And so on, and so on, until all the ice is gone.

IN THE ARCTIC, AN AREA HAS MELTED THAT'S THE SIZE OF TEXAS AND CALIFORNIA COMBINED!

CALIFORNIA

TEXAS

HOW IT LOOKS NOW

11

Ms. Frizzle steered the bus-plane
all over the earth.
We saw changes everywhere.

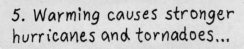
5. Warming causes stronger hurricanes and tornadoes...

...and more forest fires...

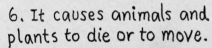
...and bigger blizzards.

GLOBAL WARMING PUTS MORE WATER IN THE AIR IN SOME PLACES. THAT MEANS MORE RAIN, AND, WHEN IT GETS COLD, MORE SNOW!

WHY IS THERE STILL COLD WEATHER?
by Keesha
Global warming means that the average temperature of the whole earth is rising.
Different places still have different weather, but, in most places, there are more hot days and fewer cold days than before.

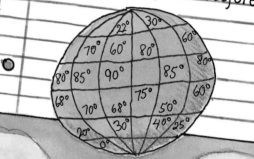

6. It causes animals and plants to die or to move.

IT'S TOO HOT HERE.

LET'S GO NORTH.

YELLOW-BELLIED MARMOTS

FIRE ANTS

7. Strange weather hurts food crops.

ICE ON AVOCADOS

THAT WHOLE CROP MIGHT BE LOST!

NO AVOCADOS? HOLY GUACAMOLE!

THE ATMOSPHERE ~ IT'S A GAS
by Phoebe

The earth is surrounded by layers of gases. All this gas is called the atmosphere.

I CALL IT AIR!

WHAT ARE GASES?
by Arnold

Gases float and fill up any space they occupy.
A gas is thinner and lighter than a solid or liquid.

ICE	WATER	STEAM
SOLID	LIQUID	GAS

GASES IN THE ATMOSPHERE
by Molly

Most of the atmosphere is made up of these two gases:

OXYGEN (O_2)

NITROGEN (N_2)

"Aren't you children wondering why the earth is getting warmer and warmer?" asked Ms. Frizzle. Actually, we were wondering why she was steering the bus-plane higher and higher.

MS. FRIZZLE, AREN'T THERE NATURAL UPS AND DOWNS IN THE CLIMATE?

YES, BUT THEY DO NOT REALLY EXPLAIN WHAT IS HAPPENING ON THE EARTH TODAY.

YAPTOP

DOES ANYTHING EXPLAIN WHAT HAPPENS IN THIS CLASS?

"Most of today's warming is caused by the increasing level of heat-trapping gases in the atmosphere," said the Friz. "Heat-trapping gases are also called greenhouse gases."
She had that funny gleam in her eye.
We could tell something "interesting" was about to happen.

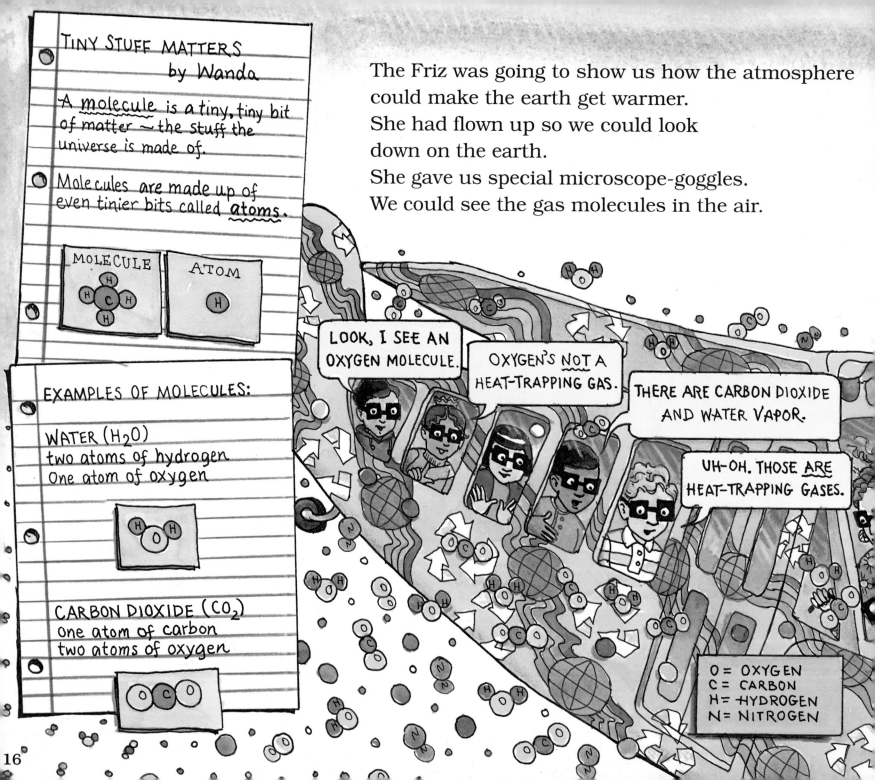

TINY STUFF MATTERS
by Wanda

A **molecule** is a tiny, tiny bit of matter ~ the stuff the universe is made of.

Molecules are made up of even tinier bits called **atoms**.

MOLECULE   ATOM

EXAMPLES OF MOLECULES:

WATER (H_2O)
two atoms of hydrogen
One atom of oxygen

CARBON DIOXIDE (CO_2)
one atom of carbon
two atoms of oxygen

The Friz was going to show us how the atmosphere could make the earth get warmer.
She had flown up so we could look down on the earth.
She gave us special microscope-goggles.
We could see the gas molecules in the air.

LOOK, I SEE AN OXYGEN MOLECULE.

OXYGEN'S NOT A HEAT-TRAPPING GAS.

THERE ARE CARBON DIOXIDE AND WATER VAPOR.

UH-OH. THOSE ARE HEAT-TRAPPING GASES.

O = OXYGEN
C = CARBON
H = HYDROGEN
N = NITROGEN

The greenhouse gases trapped some of the heat. That heat headed back to Earth again. It raised the earth's temperature even higher than before.

WHY IS GLOBAL WARMING
HAPPENING NOW?
by Tim

Humans have been on Earth for about 100,000 years. For most of that time, they didn't make enough CO_2 to change the climate.

"How can we stop global warming?" we wailed.
"One way is to use less energy," the Friz said.
"Another way is to use alternative energy!
That's energy made with less—or no—fossil fuels."

Then, about 150 years ago, people invented machines that burned fossil fuel.

Since then, more and more people have been burning more and more fossil fuels.

TODAY THERE IS 30 PERCENT MORE CO_2 IN THE ATMOSPHERE THAN THERE WAS 150 YEARS AGO.

AND MOST OF THE ADDED CO_2 CAME FROM BURNING FOSSIL FUELS.

PROPANE OIL GAS-O-LINE COAL NATURAL GAS

AND I HAVE TO DRAW MORE AND MORE CO_2 IN THE PICTURES.

22

Our teacher shooed us back on the bus-plane.
Like it or not, we were on our way to see
some alternative energy.

We set out to see generators—
machines that make electricity.
Most generators burn fossil fuel to spin
their turbines and make electricity.
Alternative generators make it without fossil fuels.

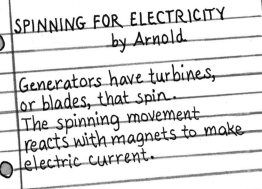

SPINNING FOR ELECTRICITY
by Arnold

Generators have turbines, or blades, that spin. The spinning movement reacts with magnets to make electric current.

TURBINE | GENERATOR

BLADES SPINNING — TURN SHAFT — SPIN MAGNETS

ELECTRIC CURRENT

LOOK AT ALL THE THINGS THAT ARE MAKING ELECTRICITY.

AND NO GREENHOUSE GASES.

HYDROELECTRIC PLANT
Movement of water over a dam spins turbines in a generator.

DAM
GENERATOR
TURBINE

GEOTHERMAL PLANT
Heat from inside the earth makes steam to move turbines.

STEAM

NUCLEAR-ELECTRIC PLANT
Heat made in nuclear reactors does the same thing.

STEAM
NUCLEAR REACTOR
COOLING TOWER

In the countryside, we saw
another alternative: windmills.
The wind turned the blades.
"Anything that moves has energy," the Friz said.
"And energy can be made into electricity."

WINDMILL

BLADES

GENERATOR

CURRENT RUNS THROUGH WIRES TO USERS.

As we flew over a desert, we heard a loud crunch.
Out the window, we saw the bus-plane's wings fall off!
"Ms. Frizzle!" we yelled, but she didn't seem to notice.
She was too busy telling us about more
alternative energy.
This time she pointed to a huge
solar generator below.

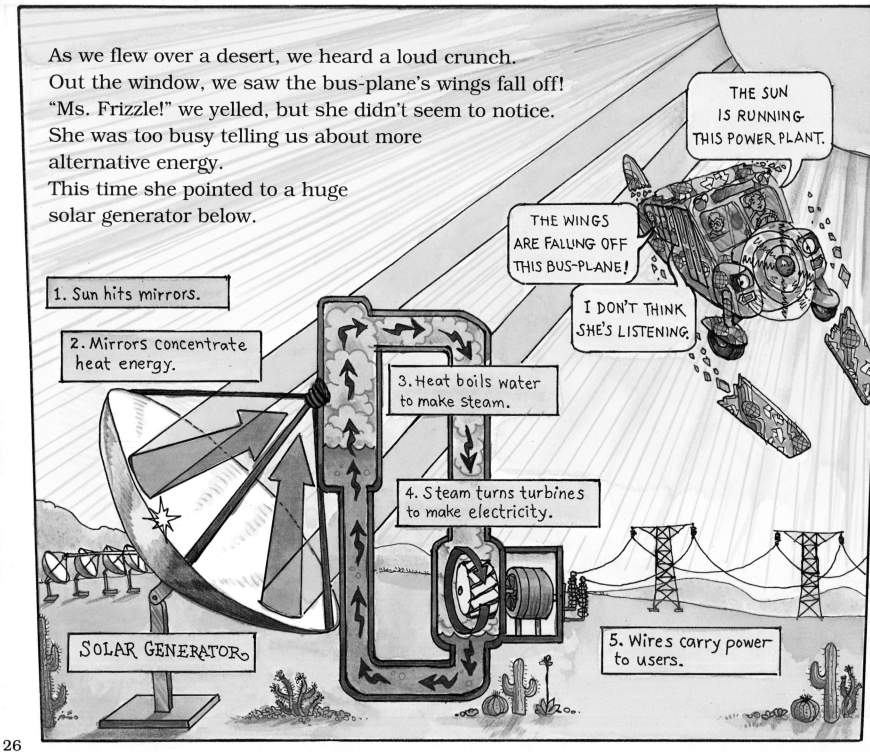

The bus made a crash landing.
Oops, we mean a *splash* landing.
We were floating in a solar-heated swimming pool.
Ms. Frizzle kept talking, telling us about solar cells.
They make energy directly from the sun—
with no moving parts.

SOLAR CELLS:
YOU ARE MY SUNSHINE
by Ralphie

Solar cells are made of special materials that make electric current when light shines on them.

The cells are microscopic. They can be put on panels or on a thin film.

CHILDREN, DO YOU NOTICE THE MANY DEVICES POWERED BY SOLAR CELLS?

UM...MS. FRIZZLE, DO YOU NOTICE THAT THE BUS IS A GIANT POOL TOY?

ROOF COVERED WITH SOLAR FILM MAKES ALL THE ELECTRICITY A FAMILY NEEDS.

Solar bags charge laptops.

WALKERVILLE TOWN POOL

HEY! NO SPLASHING!

LENNY THE LIFEGUARD

Solar panels heat pools...

...and run garden lights.

A solar "briefcase" makes energy wherever you need it.

Ms. Frizzle pulled a bright green lever. At once the bus morphed into a hybrid vehicle that ran on gasoline and a rechargeable battery.

"Can we please go back to school, Ms. Frizzle?" we begged. "We've been on this bus too long!" For once our teacher listened.

MORE WORDS FROM DOROTHY ANN

A HYBRID VEHICLE uses more than one source of energy.

A FUEL-EFFICIENT vehicle uses **less** fuel to go **more** miles.

KIDS CAN...
Take the school bus instead of being driven by a parent.

EVEN AN INEFFICIENT SCHOOL BUS EMITS LESS CO_2 THAN 20 CARS DRIVING KIDS TO SCHOOL.

KIDS CAN... Ask adults to stop letting vehicles idle.

PLEASE TURN OFF YOUR ENGINE WHILE WAITING.

We had to start saving energy right away.
"Conserve, conserve, conserve!" shouted the Friz.
"Recycle, recycle, recycle!"

I CONSERVE PAPER BY WRITING ON THE BACK.

I CONSERVE PAPER, TOO— BY NOT DOING MY HOMEWORK!

USED PAINT JARS

OLD NEWSPAPERS

RECYCLING SAVES ENERGY
by Tim

Making new cans from recycled cans uses 30% less energy than making them from new aluminum.

KIDS CAN...
Recycle cans and bottles!

CANS

BOTTLES

A LITTLE CAN DO A LOT
If your town recycled 2,000 pounds of aluminum cans, it would save enough energy to heat the typical home for 10 years.

We started making changes at our school.
There was plenty of room for improvement.
Then we called the mayor of our town.
Then we wrote to the president.

We told everyone, "Let's cut down on greenhouse gases now!"

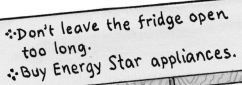

- Don't leave the fridge open too long.
- Buy Energy Star appliances.

IT'S NOT COOL TO LEAVE THE FRIDGE OPEN!

- Buy things with less packaging.
- Buying MORE local produce...

...SAVES ON PACKAGING AND TRANSPORTATION.

- Use cloth shopping bags.
- Buy LESS bottled water.

- Air-dry your laundry.

A LITTLE CAN DO A LOT

If every household in the U.S. switched three lights to compact fluorescent lamps (CFLS), it would reduce as much CO_2 as taking 3.5 million cars off the road.

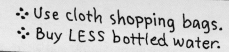

That's because old incandescent bulbs waste a lot of energy making heat. CFLS use most of their energy making light.

THE LESS ENERGY YOU USE, THE LESS CO_2 GOES INTO THE AIR.

Finally, we had time to put on our play.
It was about everything we had seen on our trip.
We showed what global warming was doing to our planet.
And we told about how people can help.

Can you believe it?
A TV station found out about us,
and we got to be on television!

35

As we left school, we asked our teacher, "Will the earth really be okay, Ms. Frizzle?"
"I hope so," said the Friz.
"Our only chance is to work together—every person, every city, every country."

39

QUESTIONS FOR MS. FRIZZLE'S CLASS
... an online chat

Q. Can a class really go up in the sky and ride sunbeams into the earth?
from IvannaNO@once.now

A. According to our research, only Ms. Frizzle's class can do that.
from Dorothy.Ann@a.loss.to.explain.net

Q. Why are you so worried about global warming? There were warm times in Earth's past, weren't there?
from Onceupon@time.now

A. In past times, Earth's climate has been cool, cold, warm, and hot. But these changes have happened over millions of years. Animals and plants had time to adjust. The warming we see now has happened in only a few hundred years. We can't adapt that fast.
from Ralphie@a.gallop.net

Q. Can a single person really change things?
from Juan@atime4change.net

A. One individual can't make a big difference.
But millions of individuals can!
from Phoebe@longlast/together.net

Q. Don't we need bigger help?
from a.giant@least?.net

A. You're right. We need all the governments of the
world to cooperate in solving the climate crisis.
from Ms.Frizzle@the.crossroads

Q. Why does Ms. Frizzle always go on such
weird class trips?
from kids@risk?safety.net

A. That's what I would like to know.
from Arnold@home.sweet.home